This Book
Belongs To:

_____

T0151070

I Do Not Like Living With BROTHERS

Written and Illustrated By
DANIEL BAXTER

I DO NOT LIKE LIVING WITH BROTHERS

Dedicated to
my sister, Mycah.

I do not like living with brothers.

Brothers always
want to go first.

And they always hog the
bathroom before school.

I never get to sit in the
front seat.

I never get to watch
the shows I want.

And don't even think about getting
a turn with video games.

My brothers never agree
with me.

And they do not listen
when I give them advice.

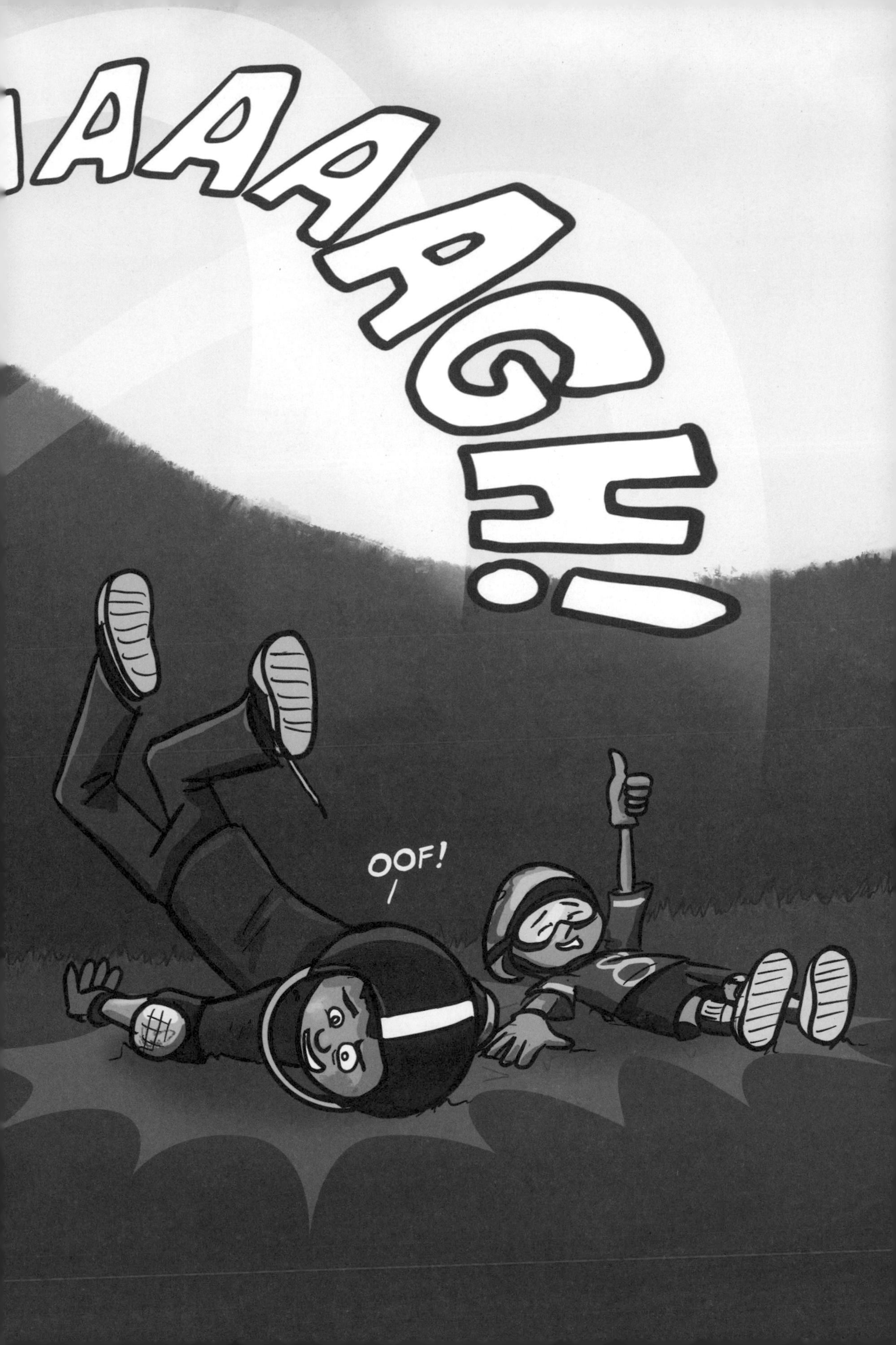
AAAAAAGH!!
OOF!

Brothers are always dirty.

And sometimes they smell!

I DO NOT LIKE LIVING WITH BROTHERS!

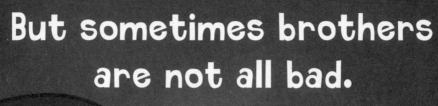

But sometimes brothers
are not all bad.

They do like to
make me laugh.

And that makes mealtime
very entertaining.

They protect me
when I am scared.

And they cheer for
me when I'm brave.

Sometimes they help me
when I need it.

And sometimes they need
me to help them.

Brothers are a lot of work.

A LOT of work.

Sometimes living with
brothers can be difficult.

But I know they love me...
and I love them too.

I guess I don't mind living
with brothers after all.